for Fafa, Florian and Sofia

Copyright © 1997 by Fulvio Testa
The rights of Fulvio Testa to be identified as the author and illustrator of this work have been asserted by him in accordance
with the Copyright, Designs and Patents Act, 1988.
First published in Great Britain in 1997 by Andersen Press Ltd., 20 Vauxhall Bridge Road, London SW1V 2SA. Published in
Australia by Random House Australia Pty., 20 Alfred Street, Milsons Point, Sydney, NSW 2061. All rights reserved.
Colour separated by Fotoriproduzioni Grafiche, Verona. Printed and bound in Italy by Grafiche AZ, Verona.

10   9   8   7   6   5   4   3   2   1

British Library Cataloguing in Publication Data available.
ISBN 0 86264 741 X

This book has been printed on acid-free paper and set in VAG Rounded Thin

A Long Trip to Z

written and illustrated by

Fulvio Testa

Andersen Press • London

A is for **a**eroplane...

Climb inside and fly out of the **b**ook,

past the bird in its **c**age,

through the crack in the **d**oor.

"Goodbye, **e**lephant! Goodbye, **f**ish!"

There is no time now to play your **g**uitar.

You fly up, up above the **h**ouse...

and far away across a desert **i**sland.

On you go. Down below a panther snoozes
in the jungle.

You fly higher than the **k**ites...

and you can see someone fishing on a lake...

or someone else climbing **m**ountains.

You fly round and round the bell tower. It is **n**oon,

and you still have far to go. What can they see from the **o**bservatory?

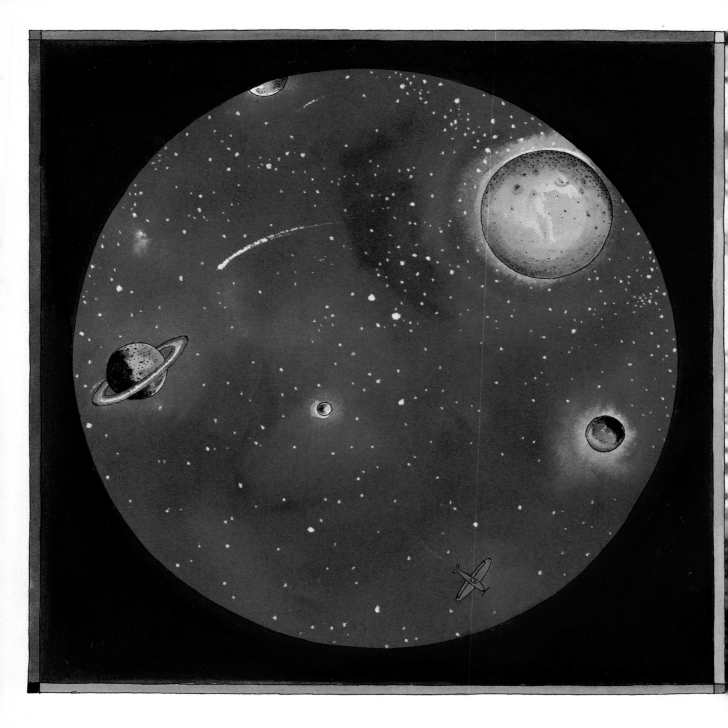

Why, you, of course, amongst the **p**lanets!

"I want to go home!" Fly in low over your bed covered with its warm **q**uilt...

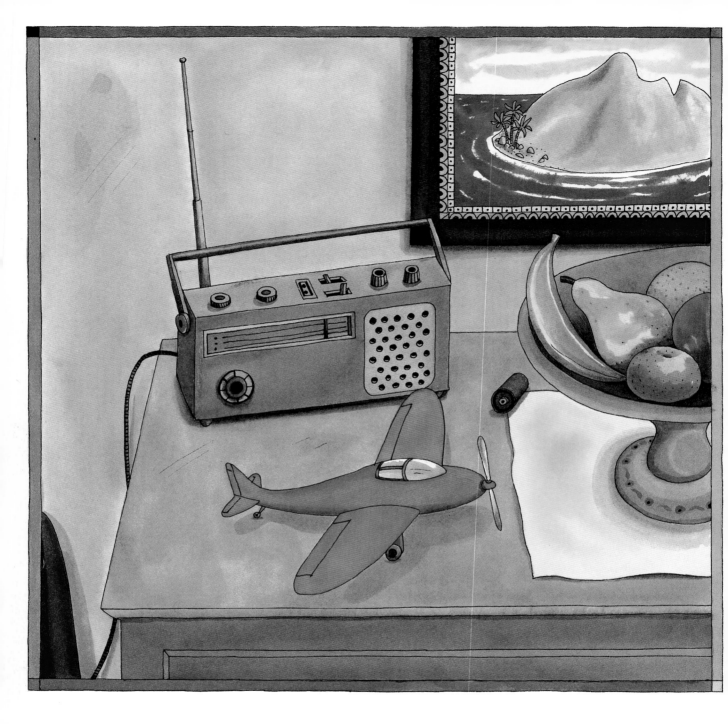

...and land safely near the **r**adio.

"Welcome back!" says Max, who is playing the **s**axophone,

and Teddy waves his **t**ambourine.

"We missed you!" says Kittycat from behind the **u**mbrella.

"Yes, it is about time you came back to your book,"
grumbles Bunny, nibbling his **v**egetables.

Look! Night has fallen - you can see it through the **w**indow.

It is too late to play your **x**ylophone and you are **y**awning.

Jump into bed and snuggle into your pillow with its pattern of galloping **z**ebras.
You have come a long way and now it is time to sleep.

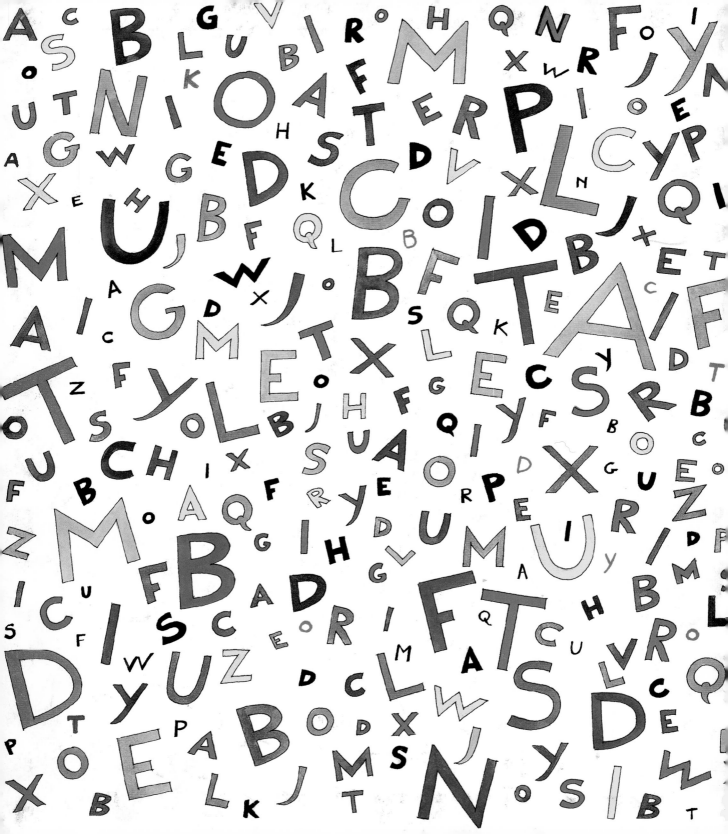

CHILLED TOMATO SOUP WITH AVOCADO CREAM

A chilled, fresh soup of puréed ripe tomatoes and mint, topped with a smooth cream flavoured with avocado. This sophisticated soup needs no cooking and is best made with flavourful Italian plum tomatoes, which provide lots of colour too. Beef tomatoes would be a good substitute, but they must be very ripe.

SERVES 6

1.4 kg (3 lb) ripe red
  tomatoes
750 ml (1¼ pints) tomato
  juice
pinch of sugar
dash of Tabasco sauce
15 ml (1 tbsp) lemon juice
30 ml (2 tbsp) chopped fresh
  mint
salt and pepper
AVOCADO CREAM
1 large ripe avocado
10-15 ml (2-3 tsp) lemon
  juice
½ small onion
30 ml (2 tbsp) chopped fresh
  mint
90 ml (6 tbsp) soured cream
TO GARNISH
mint sprigs

PREPARATION TIME
20 minutes, plus chilling
COOKING TIME
Nil
FREEZING
Suitable: soup only (with the
diced tomato); stir well when
thawed. Do not freeze the
avocado cream.

145 CALS PER SERVING

1. Halve the tomatoes, then squeeze out the seeds into a bowl. Reserve 4 tomato halves and cut into fine dice, cover and refrigerate. Strain the tomato seeds through a small sieve to extract any juices; discard the seeds.

2. Place the remaining tomatoes in a blender or food processor with all the tomato juice, the sugar, Tabasco sauce, lemon juice, chopped mint and salt and pepper to taste. Liquidise or process until smooth, then pass through a sieve into a clean bowl. Taste and adjust the seasoning.

3. Cover and leave for at least 2 hours in the refrigerator to allow the flavours to develop and the soup to become thoroughly chilled.

4. Thirty minutes before serving, halve the avocado, remove the stone, then peel. Mash the avocado flesh in a bowl, using a fork, adding lemon juice to taste. Peel and finely grate the onion and mix into the avocado with the chopped mint and soured cream.

5. Stir the reserved diced tomato into the chilled soup. Ladle the soup into individual serving bowls and add a dollop of the avocado cream to each one. Garnish with mint to serve.

VARIATION

Substitute fresh basil for the mint. Dice the avocado and stir into the soup, leaving out the grated onion. Serve topped with spoonfuls of soured cream.

TECHNIQUE

Squeeze the tomato halves over a small bowl to extract the seeds.

VICHYSSOISE WITH LEMON GRASS

This creamy, velvety soup is based on a popular classic – but with the added fragrance of oriental lemon grass. If possible, use fresh lemon grass, though you will find that dried is more readily available. To ensure a really smooth texture, it is important to liquidise and sieve the soup before serving, either hot or chilled.

SERVES 6

2 medium onions
450 g (1 lb) leeks (white part only)
175 g (6 oz) floury potatoes
1 lemon grass stalk (preferably fresh)
75 g (3 oz) butter
1.35 litres (2¼ pints) chicken stock
300 ml (½ pint) milk
150 ml (¼ pint) crème fraîche
salt and white pepper
TO SERVE
extra crème fraîche
chives, to garnish

PREPARATION TIME
15 minutes
COOKING TIME
30 minutes
FREEZING
Suitable: without the crème fraîche; add this when thoroughly thawed and reheated, whisking well

225 CALS PER SERVING

1. Peel and thinly slice the onions. Trim and slice the leeks. Peel and dice the potatoes. Bruise the lemon grass with the end of a rolling pin.

2. Melt the butter in a large saucepan and add the onions and leeks. Stir well, add 45 ml (3 tbsp) water, cover tightly and sweat over a gentle heat for 10 minutes until soft and golden.

3. Stir in the potatoes, lemon grass, chicken stock and milk. Bring to the boil, lower the heat, cover and simmer for 20 minutes until the potatoes are tender.

4. Discard the lemon grass. Allow the soup to cool slightly, then transfer to a blender or food processor and work until smooth. Pass through a sieve and return to the pan if serving hot.

5. Stir in the crème fraîche and seasoning to taste. Either cool and chill (in this case season really well) or reheat and pour into warmed soup bowls. Serve topped with a dollop of chilled crème fraîche and chives, to garnish.

NOTE: Fresh lemon grass is sold in the herb section of some supermarkets. It will freeze, but turns brown, which won't impair the flavour. Dried lemon grass is good too, as long as it isn't too old!

VARIATION

Replace the leeks with a bunch of spring onions, and add a bunch of trimmed and chopped watercress to the soup just before liquidising. The soup will be beautifully green, with a wonderful fresh taste.

TECHNIQUE

Bruise the lemon grass stalk by striking it firmly with the end of the rolling pin to release the flavour.

JERUSALEM ARTICHOKE AND PARMESAN SOUP

An unusual combination of mild Jerusalem artichokes with a hint of spice and the nutty taste of Parmesan cheese. The flavour of fresh Parmesan makes this soup really special. Don't be tempted to use the dry cheese sold in cartons – it bears no comparison to the real thing!

SERVES 6

450 g (1 lb) Jerusalem
   artichokes
2 shallots
50 g (2 oz) butter
5 ml (1 tsp) mild curry paste
900 ml (1½ pints) chicken or
   vegetable stock
150 ml (¼ pint) single
   cream (or milk for a less
   rich soup)
freshly grated nutmeg, to
   taste
pinch of cayenne pepper
60 ml (4 tbsp) freshly grated
   Parmesan cheese
salt and pepper
MELBA TOAST
3-4 slices day-old softgrain
   white bread
a little freshly grated
   Parmesan cheese, for
   sprinkling
1.25 ml (¼ tsp) paprika

PREPARATION TIME
15 minutes
COOKING TIME
25 minutes
FREEZING
Suitable

190 CALS PER SERVING

1. Scrub the Jerusalem artichokes thoroughly to remove any dirt. Pat dry, then slice thinly. Peel and dice the shallots.

2. Melt the butter in a large saucepan and add the shallots. Cook gently for 5 minutes until soft and golden. Stir in the curry paste and cook for 1 minute. Add the sliced artichokes and stock; stir well. Bring to the boil, cover and simmer for about 15 minutes or until the artichokes are tender.

3. Meanwhile, make the Melba toast. Preheat the oven to 180°C (350°F) Mark 4. Toast the bread lightly on both sides. Quickly cut off the crusts and split each slice in two. Scrape off any doughy bits, then sprinkle with Parmesan and paprika. Place on a baking sheet and bake in the oven for 10-15 minutes or until uniformly golden.

4. Add the cream, nutmeg and cayenne to the soup. Transfer to a blender or food processor and work until smooth, then pass through a sieve into a clean saucepan. Reheat the soup and stir in the Parmesan cheese. Taste and adjust the seasoning. Serve at once, with the hot Melba toast.

NOTE: If preferred the Melba toast can be prepared ahead, allowed to cool, then stored in an airtight tin. Warm through in the oven before serving.

VARIATION

Replace the Jerusalem artichokes with 1 large cauliflower. Cut away the leaves and core, and discard. Divide the cauliflower into florets. Add to the shallots with the stock and bring to the boil. Simmer for about 10 minutes or until very soft, then continue as in step 4.

TECHNIQUE

To make the Melba toast, carefully split each slice of toast horizontally in two. On baking these fine slices will curl.

14

SEARED SCALLOPS WITH ROASTED PLUM TOMATOES

This is a vibrant dish with the colours, the flavours and the simplicity I associate with Mediterranean food. Plum tomatoes are roasted to evaporate away some of their moisture, concentrating the flavour to recreate the sun-ripened sweetness of tomatoes from the Mediterranean. A simple leafy salad, some good bread and a glass of chilled wine are all I'd suggest to accompany.

SERVES 4

16 large fresh scallops,
   shelled (see page 8)
90 ml (6 tbsp) extra-virgin
   olive oil
2 garlic cloves
30 ml (2 tbsp) chopped fresh
   thyme or parsley
coarse sea salt and pepper
ROASTED TOMATOES
6 large plum tomatoes (or
   other flavourful
   tomatoes)
3 rosemary sprigs
juice of 1 small lemon

PREPARATION TIME
15 minutes
COOKING TIME
About 45 minutes
FREEZING
Not suitable

350 CALS PER SERVING

1. Preheat the oven to 180°C (350°F) Mark 4.

2. Rinse the scallops and pat dry with kitchen paper. Place in a bowl and spoon over 45 ml (3 tbsp) of the olive oil. Peel the garlic cloves and crush them to a paste on a chopping board with a little coarse sea salt. Add to the scallops with the chopped thyme or parsley. Season with pepper and mix well. Cover and refrigerate while preparing the tomatoes.

3. Cut the tomatoes lengthwise in half. Place them in one layer, cut side up, in a shallow baking tin. Add the rosemary and season liberally with sea salt. Drizzle over the remaining olive oil. Roast in the preheated oven for about 45 minutes until tender but still holding their shape.

4. About 10 minutes before the tomatoes are ready, preheat a large dry (not oiled) cast-iron griddle pan over a high heat for approximately 5 minutes. Lower the heat to medium.

5. To cook the scallops add them to the hot griddle pan in one layer. Allow to sizzle undisturbed for 1½ minutes, then turn each scallop and cook the other side for 1½ minutes.

6. To serve, lift the tomatoes from the baking tin and arrange on four warmed serving plates with the scallops and rosemary sprigs.

7. Tip the oil from the tomatoes into the griddle pan and add the lemon juice. Stir well and scrape up all the flavoursome sediment in the bottom of the pan as it sizzles. Trickle the juices over the scallops and roasted plum tomatoes and serve at once.

NOTE: A large griddle pan will take all of the scallops in a single layer, but if your pan is smaller you may need to cook them in two batches.

TECHNIQUE

Arrange the tomato halves, cut side up, in one layer in a shallow baking tin. Add the rosemary, sprinkle with sea salt and drizzle with olive oil before baking.

CHICKEN BREASTS WITH SPINACH AND RICOTTA

Tender chicken breasts are stuffed with a well-seasoned ricotta filling, then wrapped in fresh spinach leaves and poached in wine until tender. The cooking juices are reduced to form a delicate sauce which is 'mounted' with a little butter for gloss. A pale and pretty dish – full of fresh, clean flavours – which is ideal served with crunchy-topped asparagus and courgettes (page 54).

SERVES 4

4 boneless chicken breasts,
  skinned
50 g (2 oz) frozen chopped
  spinach, thawed
175 g (6 oz) ricotta cheese
60 ml (4 tbsp) freshly grated
  Parmesan cheese
freshly grated nutmeg
salt and pepper
8 large fresh spinach leaves
150 ml (¼ pint) dry white
  wine
300 ml (½ pint) chicken
  stock
50 g (2 oz) butter, chilled
  and diced

PREPARATION TIME
30 minutes
COOKING TIME
30-40 minutes
FREEZING
Not suitable

400 CALS PER SERVING

1. Using a sharp knife, make a deep horizontal slit in each chicken breast through the thicker side, to make a pocket.

2. Squeeze the moisture out of the thawed spinach, then place in a bowl. Add the ricotta, Parmesan and plenty of nutmeg, salt and pepper. Mix well, then spoon the filling evenly into the chicken pockets.

3. Trim the stems from the fresh spinach. Bring a pan of salted water to the boil and add the spinach leaves. Immediately remove with a slotted spoon and plunge into a bowl of cold water to set the colour and prevent further cooking. Wrap two spinach leaves around each chicken breast. Tie with thin cotton string to secure.

4. Lay the chicken breasts in a wide shallow pan or flameproof casserole and pour in the wine and stock. Bring to the boil, lower the heat, cover and simmer gently for 30-40 minutes until cooked. Remove the chicken breasts from the pan with a slotted spoon and keep warm.

5. Boil the cooking liquid rapidly until reduced by half. Take off the heat and whisk in the cubed butter, to enrich the sauce and give it a shine. Taste and adjust the seasoning.

6. To serve, slice the chicken breasts and arrange on warmed serving plates with a little sauce. Serve the remaining sauce separately.

NOTE: Another type of curd cheese or soft cream cheese can be used in place of the ricotta.

TECHNIQUE

Cut a deep pocket in each chicken breast, then spoon in the spinach and ricotta filling, dividing it equally between them.

46

Duck Breasts With Rösti And Apple

Rosy pink, tender slices of 'roasted' duck breast are served on golden apple and potato cakes and accompanied by sautéed caramelised apple slices. The method used to cook the duck breasts encourages most of the fat to run out and the skin becomes deliciously crisp and brown. If possible buy the large French *magrets* – one of these easily serves two. Otherwise you will need four standard sized duck breasts.

SERVES 4

2 large duck breast fillets,
   each about 350 g (12 oz),
   or 4 medium duck breast
   fillets (at room
   temperature)
salt and pepper
15 ml (1 tbsp) red wine
   vinegar
60 ml (4 tbsp) apple juice
RÖSTI
2 large old potatoes, about
   450 g (1 lb) total weight
1 dessert apple
2 fresh sage leaves
oil, for frying
TO GARNISH
sautéed apple slices
sage sprigs

PREPARATION TIME
30 minutes
COOKING TIME
20-25 minutes
FREEZING
Not suitable

430 CALS PER SERVING

1. Use a sharp knife to score through the skin side of the duck. Rub with salt and pepper. Leave at room temperature for 15 minutes.

2. To make the rösti, peel and finely grate the potatoes and apple. Squeeze out as much moisture as possible and place in a bowl. Chop the sage and mix with the potato and apple. Season well with salt and pepper.

3. Preheat the oven to 150°C (300°F) Mark 2. Heat 15 ml (1 tbsp) oil in a small heavy-based frying pan. Place 2 large tablespoonfuls of the potato mixture in the pan, pressing down hard with a fish slice. Cook for 2 minutes or until golden brown on the underside; turn over and cook until crisp and golden. Remove and drain on kitchen paper. Repeat with the remaining mixture until you have at least 8 rösti. Keep warm in the oven while cooking the duck.

4. Preheat a heavy flameproof casserole. Add the duck breasts skin-side down and cook over a medium heat for 7-10 minutes depending on size, without moving them; the fat that runs out will prevent them sticking. Turn the breasts over and cook for 3-4 minutes, depending on size.

5. Using a slotted spoon, transfer the duck breasts to a warmed serving dish. Cover and leave in the warm oven for 10 minutes to relax and become evenly 'rosy' inside. Meanwhile pour of all the fat from the pan. Add the wine vinegar and apple juice. Bring to the boil and reduce slightly.

6. To serve, place two rösti on each warmed serving plate. Slice the duck thickly and arrange evenly on top of the rösti. Spoon on the sauce and serve immediately, garnished with sautéed apple slices and sage.

TECHNIQUE

Score through the skin of each duck breast on the diagonal, using a sharp knife. This encourages the fat to run out and the skin to crisp on cooking.

CHAR-GRILLED SPATCHCOCK POUSSINS

Spatchcocked poussins make an unusual change from roast chicken. The poussin or baby chicken is split and flattened enabling it to be grilled evenly. Ready-prepared spatchcocked poussins are widely available in supermarkets, but you can always prepare them yourself if preferred (see step-by-step instructions on page 9). Brushed with a honey and lemon glaze, the skin becomes shiny, partly charred and crisp – with a lemony tang. Stir-fried summer vegetables (page 60) are an excellent accompaniment.

SERVES 4

2 or 4 ready-prepared
   spatchcock poussins (see
   note)
finely grated rind and juice
   of 1 lemon
60 ml (4 tbsp) thin honey
30 ml (2 tbsp) Dijon
   mustard
30 ml (2 tbsp) dark soy
   sauce
5 ml (1 tsp) mild paprika
salt and pepper

PREPARATION TIME
15 minutes
COOKING TIME
20-30 minutes
FREEZING
Not suitable

330 CALS PER SERVING

1. Preheat the grill to medium. Place the poussins skin-side down on a grill rack.

2. In a bowl, mix the lemon juice with the honey, mustard, soy sauce, paprika and seasoning to make the glaze.

3. Brush the poussins all over with the glaze and grill for 10 minutes, brushing with more glaze as necessary. Turn over carefully and brush with glaze. Grill for 10-20 minutes until the poussins are cooked through and the juices from the thigh run clear, not pink (see note). The skin will be well-charred while the meat underneath should be perfectly tender.

4. Remove any skewers from the poussins. If using larger poussins, split in two along the length of the breast bone. Serve the poussins with any pan juices poured over, accompanied by stir-fried summer vegetables.

NOTE: If you buy small poussins, you will need to allow one per person. Larger poussins will serve two, but may take longer to cook through. If necessary lower the grill pan to prevent the skin from over-blackening.

VARIATION

In place of poussins, use chicken joints or even chicken breasts – corn-fed ones have a particularly good flavour.

TECHNIQUE

Brush the poussins all over with the lemon and honey glaze before – and during – grilling.

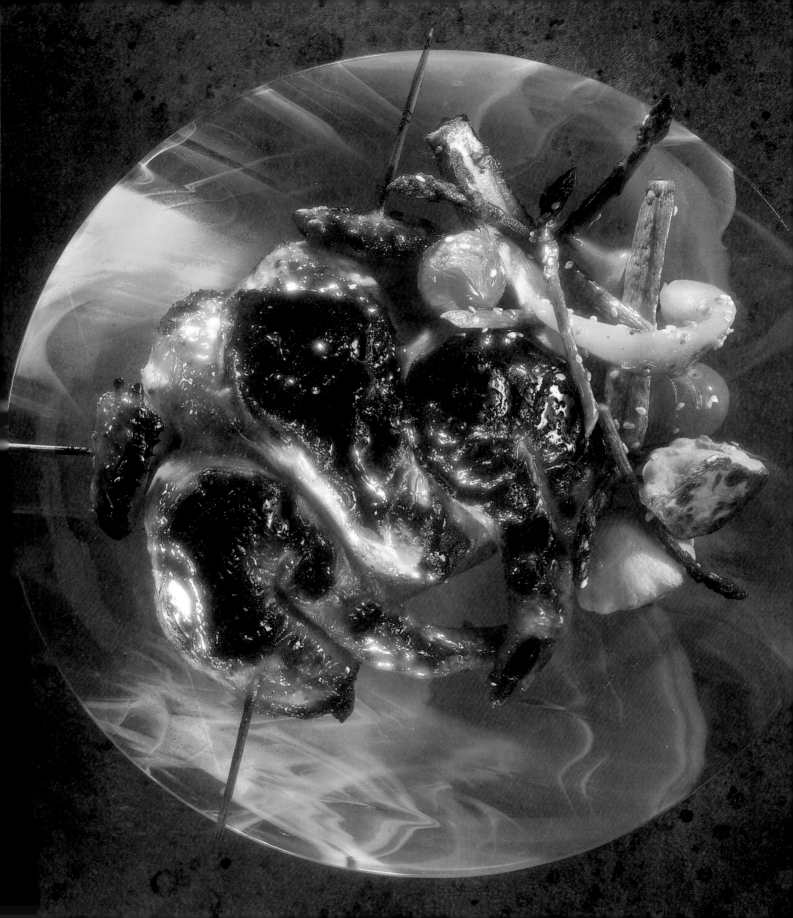

BITTER GREEN SALAD WITH CITRUS DRESSING

A delicious crunchy, slightly peppery salad to accompany rich meats, or to serve as a separate salad course. The piquant dressing adds a mellow sweetness to the sharp leaves – but remember to apply it just before serving otherwise the salad will become limp. Bitter leaves are becoming more readily available in supermarkets today – look out for new varieties and experiment!

SERVES 4

225 g (8 oz) mixed bitter salad leaves, such as rocket, watercress, batavia, sorrel, young spinach

CITRUS DRESSING

I orange

I lime

30 ml (2 tbsp) sunflower oil

15 ml (1 tbsp) walnut oil

15 ml (1 tbsp) dark soy sauce

15 ml (1 tbsp) thin honey

salt and pepper

PREPARATION TIME
15 minutes
COOKING TIME
Nil
FREEZING
Not suitable

125 CALS PER SERVING

I. Wash all the salad leaves and tear into smaller pieces if necessary. Spin dry in a salad spinner, then transfer to a plastic bag with any water still clinging to the leaves. Store in the refrigerator for about 30 minutes to crisp up the salad.

2. To make the dressing, finely grate the rind from the orange and lime. Squeeze the juice from both fruit. Place 15 ml (1 tbsp) each grated rind in a small bowl with 30 ml (2 tbsp) orange juice and 15 ml (1 tbsp) lime juice. Add the oils, soy sauce and honey, and whisk well. Taste and check the seasoning. Just before serving the salad, strain the dressing through a fine sieve.

3. To serve, place the salad leaves in a bowl and pour over the dressing. Toss well and serve immediately.

NOTE: Rocket is expensive to buy, but grows like a weed in the garden. Try planting some – it will even grow in a window box!

VARIATION

Make the salad with chicory leaves and radicchio for a more colourful version. Add sprigs of herbs, such as basil, chervil, dill and tarragon.

TECHNIQUE

Wash the salad leaves under cold running water and tear any larger ones into smaller pieces.

CRUNCHY-TOPPED ASPARAGUS AND COURGETTES

This is a really quick and simple way of serving seasonal vegetables. The crunchy breadcrumb and Parmesan topping provides an excellent contrast to the melting texture of the asparagus and courgettes. Try it with other vegetables too, such as broccoli or cauliflower.

SERVES 4-6

225 g (8 oz) thin asparagus
225 g (8 oz) baby courgettes
salt and pepper
125 g (4 oz) butter
175 g (6 oz) fresh white
  breadcrumbs
50 g (2 oz) freshly grated
  Parmesan cheese

PREPARATION TIME
15 minutes
COOKING TIME
5-6 minutes
FREEZING
Not suitable

445-300 CALS PER SERVING

1. Trim the asparagus and cut into 5 cm (2 inch) lengths. Cut the courgettes into quarters lengthways. Bring a pan of salted water to the boil. Drop in the asparagus and courgettes, return to the boil and cook for 3 minutes. Drain and refresh immediately in cold water to stop the cooking. Remove and drain on kitchen paper.

2. Heat the butter in a frying pan and fry the breadcrumbs until lightly golden and crisp. Stir in the Parmesan cheese.

3. Preheat the grill. Place the asparagus and courgettes in a warmed shallow flameproof dish. Cover thickly with the crumbs and place under the grill for 2-3 minutes or until the topping is golden and the vegetables are heated through. Serve immediately.

VARIATION

Replace the asparagus and/or courgettes with any other green vegetable – try broccoli florets, cauliflower, French beans, or even carrots, but be sure to half-cook them before adding the topping.

TECHNIQUE

To quickly stop the vegetables cooking, remove from the boiling water and briefly immerse in a bowl of cold water. The easiest way to do this is to contain the vegetables in a blanching basket during cooking.

GRILLED CHICORY AND RADICCHIO WITH ORANGE

Grilling the chicory and radicchio transforms them by caramelising the juices – and the addition of creamy, fresh British goat's cheese gives this recipe true dinner-party status! Any other cheese will do, but the goat's cheese seems to have a special affinity with bitter leaves like chicory and radicchio. Serve this accompaniment with roast or grilled meats or poultry.

SERVES 4

2 plump heads of chicory
1 large firm head of
   radicchio
1 orange
olive oil, for basting
125 g (4 oz) fresh goat's
   cheese
a little chopped fresh or
   dried thyme
pepper
30 ml (2 tbsp) pine nuts

PREPARATION TIME
15 minutes
COOKING TIME
About 10 minutes
FREEZING
Not suitable

230 CALS PER SERVING

1. Cut the chicory in half lengthways. Cut the radicchio into quarters. Over a bowl to catch the juice, peel the orange of all pith and cut into segments, discarding the membrane.

2. Preheat the grill to high. Place the chicory and radicchio in a grill pan, cut side up, and brush liberally with olive oil. Cook under the grill, as near to the heat as possible, for about 3-4 minutes until just beginning to char and soften. Turn, baste with more olive oil and cook for a further 2-3 minutes.

3. Carefully turn the chicory and radicchio again. Arrange the orange segments on top and sprinkle with the reserved orange juice. Crumble the goat's cheese on top. Brush with oil, sprinkle with thyme and season with pepper. Grill until the cheese bubbles and begins to brown. The chicory will be very soft, so carefully transfer it to warmed plates. Alternatively, transfer to a flameproof serving dish before adding the cheese, then grill in the dish.

4. Meanwhile toast the pine nuts in a dry pan over moderate heat, shaking the pan constantly, until evenly golden. Sprinkle the toasted nuts over the grilled chicory and radicchio, to serve.

NOTE: The chicory and radicchio will change colour, but don't worry – they will taste delicious – as long as you use olive oil for basting.

VARIATION

Omit the goat's cheese and top with orange slices instead of segments.

TECHNIQUE

Peel the orange (as you would an apple) over a bowl to catch the juice, making sure you remove all of the white pith.

SWEET POTATO AND CHESTNUT CAKES WITH SPRING ONIONS

Chestnuts and sweet potatoes have a natural affinity as you will discover on tasting these unusual patties. Avoid using canned chestnuts in brine – they will be too watery. The crisp-fried cakes are best served with game and rich dark meat dishes. Alternatively try serving them on their own with a tomato sauce.

SERVES 4-6

450 g (1 lb) sweet potatoes
   (see note)
225 g (8 oz) vacuum-packed
   chestnuts
6 spring onions
75 g (3 oz) butter
30 ml (2 tbsp) chopped fresh
   parsley
2.5 ml (½ tsp) ground mace
salt and pepper
flour, for coating
1 (size 1) egg, beaten
125 g (4 oz) fresh white
   breadcrumbs
sunflower oil, for shallow-
   frying
TO GARNISH
parsley sprigs

PREPARATION TIME
30 minutes, plus chilling
COOKING TIME
30 minutes
FREEZING
Suitable: Stage 4

570 -380 CALS PER SERVING

1. Peel the sweet potatoes and cut into large chunks. Place in a steamer and steam for 15-20 minutes until tender. Remove the basket from the steamer and allow the potatoes to rest for 2-3 minutes to allow excess moisture to evaporate.

2. Place the potatoes and chestnuts in a bowl and mash until smooth. Trim and slice the spring onions.

3. Heat the butter in a frying pan and add the spring onions. Fry for 1 minute until beginning to soften, then add to the potato with the parsley and mix well. Season with the mace, and salt and pepper to taste. Work the ingredients until the mixture comes together.

4. Divide the mixture into eight and roll each portion into a ball. Flatten each one to make a thick cake. Transfer to a baking sheet and chill in the refrigerator for at least 30 minutes.

5. Season a little flour and use to lightly coat the cakes. Dip each one into beaten egg and finally coat with the breadcrumbs. Chill in the refrigerator for 30 minutes to set.

6. Heat a 1 cm (½ inch) depth of oil in a frying pan until a breadcrumb dropped into the pan sizzles in 30 seconds. Fry the cakes in batches on both sides until golden. Drain on kitchen paper. Serve immediately, garnished with parsley.

NOTE: There are two kinds of sweet potato – one has a purply skin and orange flesh, the other has a brown skin and white flesh. Both taste good but the orange-fleshed variety has the edge.

VARIATION

For a less rich version, use plain mashed potato instead of the sweet potato.

TECHNIQUE

Roll each piece into a ball in the palm of your hand, then flatten to form a cake.

STIR-FRIED SUMMER VEGETABLES

This colourful stir-fry has the sweet-sour taste of balsamic vinegar which brings out the earthy sweetness of the vegetables. Those suggested here are just a selection of the vegetables available throughout the summer: try other combinations, but always blanch or par-cook harder ones first.

SERVES 4-6

1 large yellow pepper
125 g (4 oz) baby courgettes
125 g (4 oz) patty pan
   squashes (optional)
125 g (4 oz) baby carrots
125 g (4 oz) fine asparagus
2 garlic cloves
15 ml (1 tbsp) vegetable oil
15 ml (1 tbsp) olive oil
125 g (4 oz) cherry
   tomatoes
75 ml (3 fl oz) chicken or
   vegetable stock or canned
   consommé (see note)
salt and pepper
30 ml (2 tbsp) balsamic or
   sherry vinegar
5 ml (1 tbsp) sesame oil
TO GARNISH
15 ml (1 tbsp) toasted
   sesame seeds

PREPARATION TIME
15 minutes
COOKING TIME
7-8 minutes
FREEZING
Not suitable

160-110 CALS PER SERVING

1. Halve the pepper, remove the core and seeds, then cut into long triangular shapes. Halve the courgettes lengthways. If using patty pans, cut them in half. Trim the carrots and peel if necessary, leaving on a tuft of stalk. Trim the asparagus spears. Peel and roughly chop the garlic.

2. Bring a pan of salted water to the boil. Add the yellow pepper and carrots and blanch for 2 minutes, then remove with a slotted spoon and plunge into a bowl of cold water to stop the cooking and preserve the colour. Drain well on kitchen paper.

3. Heat a wok or deep frying pan until smoking, swirl in the vegetable and olive oils and add the garlic. Stir-fry for 20 seconds, then add all the vegetables and stir-fry for 1 minute. Pour in the stock and season with salt and pepper. Stir-fry for 3-4 minutes until the vegetables are just tender.

4. Sprinkle over the balsamic vinegar and sesame oil, stir and transfer to a warmed serving dish. Sprinkle with the sesame seeds and serve immediately.

NOTE: Canned consommé is a good substitute for small amounts of stock as it imparts plenty of flavour and 'body'.

VARIATION

For a winter vegetable stir-fry, use equal quantities of cauliflower florets, broccoli florets and carrot sticks, plus 2-3 spring onions, sliced, and a little chopped fresh root ginger.

TECHNIQUE

Toss the vegetables constantly over a high heat to ensure they cook quickly, retaining their colour and a crisp texture.

POTATO PARSNIP GALETTE

This golden cake of butter-basted potatoes and sweet parsnips with a hint of honey and lemon is a perfect partner to roasts and game dishes. It is really important to clarify the butter – as it lends a wonderful colour to the potatoes and intensifies the flavour.

SERVES 6

900 g (2 lb) firm potatoes,
   such as Desirée, Romano,
   Estima or Wilja
225 g (8 oz) young parsnips
175 g (6 oz) unsalted butter
60 ml (4 tbsp) thin honey
30 ml (2 tbsp) lemon juice
freshly grated nutmeg
salt and pepper

PREPARATION TIME
25 minutes
COOKING TIME
45 minutes
FREEZING
Not suitable

380 CALS PER SERVING

1. Preheat the oven to 200°C (400°F) Mark 6. Peel the potatoes and parsnips. Slice them very thinly either by hand, with a mandoline, or in a food processor. Do not rinse the potatoes to remove the starch as it is needed to help the potato slices stick together. Divide the potatoes into three equal portions. Don't worry if they discolour.

2. To clarify the butter, slowly melt it in a small pan, then skim off any white residue or foam; keep warm. Melt the honey and lemon juice together in a small pan; keep warm.

3. Pour 30 ml (2 tbsp) butter into a heavy 20 cm (8 inch) non-stick frying pan, suitable for oven use (see note). Layer one third of the potatoes over the bottom of the pan in neat overlapping circles, seasoning well.

4. Lay half the sliced parsnips over the potato layer. Brush with honey and lemon juice and season with nutmeg, salt and pepper.

5. Cover with another third of the potato slices, brushing with butter and seasoning well as you go. Layer the remaining parsnips on top. Brush with the remaining honey and lemon juice, and season with nutmeg, salt and pepper. Finish with the remaining potato slices, brushing with butter and seasoning. Pour over any remaining butter.

6. Place the pan over a medium heat and cook carefully for about 5 minutes or until the underside begins to turn golden brown. Test by carefully lifting up the edge with a palette knife.

7. Press the potatoes down firmly and cover with a lid or buttered kitchen foil. Bake for 40-45 minutes or until the potatoes and parsnips are tender when pierced with a sharp knife and the underside is a deep golden brown.

8. Loosen the galette with a palette knife. Place a warmed serving plate over the pan and quickly invert the galette onto the dish. Serve immediately.

NOTE: Ideally you need a non-stick frying pan with an integral metal handle which can therefore be placed in the oven. Alternatively, use a moule á manqué pan instead, buttering it well.

TECHNIQUE

Layer the potato slices over the parsnips in neat, overlapping circles.

STEAMED BASIL AND MUSTARD SEED RICE

Wonderfully fragrant, this rice is a little sticky, but great for mopping up juices. It goes equally well with fish, meat or game. Black mustard seeds impart a nutty flavour to the rice without being too hot. You can, however, use yellow mustard seeds as an alternative – for a hotter flavour.

SERVES 4

225 g (8 oz) basmati rice
12 large basil leaves
30 ml (2 tbsp) sunflower oil
30 ml (2 tbsp) black
   mustard seeds
5 ml (1 tsp) salt
TO GARNISH
basil leaves

PREPARATION TIME
10 minutes
COOKING TIME
25 minutes
FREEZING
Not suitable

270 CALS PER SERVING

1. Wash the rice in several changes of cold water or in a sieve under cold running water until the water runs clear. Drain well. Shred the basil leaves or tear into pieces.

2. Heat the oil in a medium non-stick saucepan and add the mustard seeds. Cook for a few minutes until the seeds start to pop.

3. Stir in the rice, salt and 300 ml (½ pint) water. Bring to the boil, stir, then boil rapidly until the water has evaporated and there are steam holes all over the surface.

4. Stir in all but 15 ml (1 tbsp) of the basil and cover very tightly, so no steam can escape. Set on a simmering mat (see note) over a very low heat for 15 minutes for the rice to swell. Fluff up with a fork, adding the reserved basil. Serve immediately, garnished with basil leaves.

NOTE: A simmering mat is used here to ensure the heat is *very* low and evenly distributed. You can obtain one of these mats from a cookshop or hardware store. If you do not have one make sure the heat is kept to a minimum and add a little more water if necessary to prevent the rice sticking.

VARIATION

Use multi-grain rice, but allow longer to cook: fast boil with 450 ml (¾ pint) water until evaporated, then continue as above.

TECHNIQUE

Wash the basmati rice thoroughly, running the grains through your fingers, to remove excess starch.

TIRAMISU TORTE

An outrageously rich cheesecake with an irresistible soft gooey texture, based on the delicious ingredients of Tiramisu – coffee, mascarpone, chocolate, coffee liqueur and rum. A creamy rum and vanilla mixture is marbled into a dark chocolate, coffee and liqueur mixture, poured into an amaretti biscuit shell and baked. The torte is then cooled and chilled thoroughly before serving.

SERVES 8-10

BISCUIT CASE
275 g (10 oz) amaretti
   biscuits, ratafias or
   macaroons
125 g (4 oz) unsalted butter
FILLING
700 g (1½ lb) mascarpone
   or Philadelphia cream
   cheese (at room
   temperature)
150 g (5 oz) caster sugar
3 eggs, separated
30 g (1 oz) plain flour
45 ml (3 tbsp) dark rum
2.5 ml (½ tsp) vanilla
   essence
175 g (6 oz) plain dark
   chocolate
15 ml (1 tbsp) finely ground
   espresso coffee
45 ml (3 tbsp) Tia Maria or
   other coffee liqueur
TO FINISH
icing sugar, for dusting
   (optional)

PREPARATION TIME
40 minutes, plus chilling
COOKING TIME
45 minutes
FREEZING
Suitable

910-735 CALS PER SERVING

1. Place the biscuits in a blender or food processor and process until finely ground. Melt 75 g (3 oz) unsalted butter and stir in the crumbs until well coated. Spoon into a 23 cm (9 inch) loose-bottomed springform cake tin. Press evenly over the base and 4 cm (1½ inches) up the sides with the back of a spoon to form a neat shell. Chill for at least 30 minutes until firm.

2. Preheat the oven to 200°C (400°F) Mark 6. Using a wooden spoon or in an electric mixer, beat the cream cheese until smooth. Add the sugar and beat again until smooth, then beat in the egg yolks. Divide the mixture in half and stir the flour, rum and vanilla into one half.

3. Melt the chocolate in a bowl over a pan of simmering water, cool slightly, then stir in the coffee and coffee liqueur. Stir into the remaining half of the cheese mixture. Whisk the egg whites until just holding soft peaks and fold half into each flavoured cheese mixture.

4. Quickly spoon alternate mounds of the two cheese mixtures into the set biscuit case until full. Using a knife, swirl the mixtures together to produce a marbled effect.

5. Bake in the oven for 45 minutes, covering the top with foil if it appears to be over-browning. At this stage the torte

will be soft in the middle. Leave in the switched-off oven with the door slightly ajar, to cool completely; it will continue to firm up during this time. Chill for several hours before serving, to allow the flavours to develop.

6. If preferred, dust the top of the cheesecake with icing sugar. Serve cut into wedges, with crème fraîche if desired.

NOTE: Use a potato masher to press the crumbs evenly over the base of the loose-bottomed cake tin.

VARIATION

Substitute an equal quantity of chocolate digestives for the amaretti biscuits and proceed in the same way.

TECHNIQUE

Using the end of a sharp knife, swirl the two different flavoured cheese mixtures together to produce a marbled pattern.

WALNUT TART WITH CARAMEL ICE CREAM

Walnuts and caramel are a marriage made in heaven! Walnuts are encased in an irresistible gooey fudge mixture in this tart. The accompanying soft caramel ice cream is easy to make and does not require stirring during freezing. Watch that the caramel doesn't become too dark or the ice cream will be bitter.

SERVES 8-10

CARAMEL ICE CREAM
225 g (8 oz) granulated
   sugar
300 ml (½ pint) milk
300 ml (½ pint) double
   cream
8 egg yolks
PASTRY
225 g (8 oz) plain white flour
30 ml (2 tbsp) icing sugar
125 g (4 oz) butter
2 egg yolks
FILLING
125 g (4 oz) unsalted butter,
   softened
125 g (4 oz) light soft brown
   sugar
3 eggs
finely grated rind and juice
   of 1 small orange
175 g (6 oz) golden syrup
225 g (8 oz) shelled walnut
   pieces
pinch of salt

PREPARATION TIME
1 hour, plus freezing
COOKING TIME
1 hour
FREEZING
Suitable

1065-850 CALS PER SERVING

1. To make the ice cream, put the sugar in a saucepan with 150 ml (¼ pint) water. Dissolve over a low heat until clear. Increase the heat and boil rapidly until the sugar begins to caramelise.

2. Remove from the heat and leave the caramel to stand for 2-3 minutes; it will turn a deep amber brown colour. Pour on the milk and cream, stirring (see technique); then whisk in the egg yolks. Return to a gentle heat and stir, without letting the custard boil, for about 15 minutes until slightly thickened. Allow to cool, then chill.

3. Freeze the ice cream, using an ice cream machine if you have one. Alternatively, pour the mixture into a freezer-proof container and freeze until firm.

4. To make the pastry, sift the flour and icing sugar together into a bowl and rub in the butter. Stir in the egg yolks and enough iced water to bind to a firm dough. Knead lightly until smooth. Wrap in cling film and chill for 30 minutes.

5. Preheat the oven to 200°C (400°F) Mark 6. Roll out the pastry thinly and use to line a 23 cm (9 inch) fluted flan tin. Chill for 20 minutes. Line with greaseproof paper and baking beans and bake blind for 15-20 minutes, removing

the paper and beans for the last 5 minutes. Reduce the oven setting to 180°C (350°F) Mark 4.

6. To make the filling, cream the butter and sugar together until light and fluffy. Gradually beat in the eggs, one at a time, then stir in the orange rind and juice. Heat the syrup until runny, but not very hot, then stir into the filling with the walnuts and salt. Pour into the flan case and bake for 40-45 minutes until lightly browned and risen. (The tart will sink a little on cooling.) Serve warm or cold, in slices with a scoop of caramel ice cream.

NOTE: The ice cream will always be a little soft owing to the high quantity of sugar. Serve straight from the freezer.

TECHNIQUE

Carefully pour the milk and cream onto the caramel, stirring. The mixture almost sets at this stage, but dissolves on heating.

TWO-CHOCOLATE LACE PANCAKES

Dark, chocolate-flavoured lacy pancakes are filled with a rich white chocolate mousse, then served dusted with cocoa and icing sugar on a lake of single cream. You will find that a little of the filling goes a long way. Try rolling and folding the pancakes in different ways.

PANCAKES
125 g (4 oz) plain white
    flour, less 30 ml (2 tbsp)
30 ml (2 tbsp) cocoa powder
15 ml (1 tbsp) icing sugar
pinch of salt
1 egg, plus 1 egg yolk
300 ml (½ pint) milk
15 ml (1 tbsp) sunflower oil
a little extra oil, for cooking
CHOCOLATE MOUSSE
250 g (9 oz) quality white
    chocolate (see note)
30 ml (2 tbsp) Grand
    Marnier or other orange-
    flavoured liqueur
350 ml (12 fl oz) double
    cream
TO SERVE
150 ml (¼ pint) single
    cream
cocoa powder, for dusting
icing sugar, for dusting

PREPARATION TIME
45 minutes, plus chilling
COOKING TIME
2 minutes per pancake
FREEZING
Suitable: Pancakes only
(interleaved with greaseproof)

715 CALS PER SERVING

1. Place all the ingredients for the pancakes in a blender or food processor and work until smooth. Pour into a jug and leave to rest in a cool place for at least 30 minutes.

2. Heat a 15 cm (6 inch) crêpe pan until very hot and wipe with a little oil. (The hotter the pan the lacier your crêpes will be). Pour in about 30 ml (2 tbsp) batter, quickly swirling it around the pan. Don't worry if there are small holes in the pancake – they will look good in the final version! As soon as it sets, turn over and cook the other side. Transfer to a warmed plate and continue until all the batter is used up, heating the pan well each time and interleaving the cooked pancakes with greaseproof paper to prevent them sticking. You should have sufficient batter for 12 pancakes.

3. To make the mousse, chop the chocolate into tiny pieces and place in a heatproof bowl with the liqueur and 45 ml (3 tbsp) water. Stand over a pan of hot water and stir constantly until the chocolate is melted and smooth. Allow to cool until tepid.

4. Whisk the cream until it forms soft peaks and fold into the chocolate mixture. Working quickly – as the mousse sets fast – place 30 ml (2 tbsp) on each pancake and roll or fold carefully to enclose the filling. Place on a tray as you go. Chill for at least 1 hour.

5. To serve, pour a little single cream onto each serving plate and place two pancakes on top. Dust liberally with cocoa powder, then icing sugar. Serve immediately.

NOTE: Use only white chocolate that has been made with pure cocoa butter for optimum flavour and texture. Lindt and Tobler are both suitable brands. The pancakes should look delicate when filled – don't make them too large!

TECHNIQUE

Fold each lacy pancake around 30 ml (2 tbsp) of the mousse filling, working as quickly as possible.

COCONUT BAVAROIS WITH TROPICAL FRUIT SAUCE

A pretty pale creamy moulded custard, flecked with little specks of vanilla, cloaked and floating on a golden sea of mango and passion fruit sauce. The truly tropical tastes of coconut, mango and passion fruit are given a lift by using coconut liqueur and orange and lime juice.

SERVES 6

400 ml (14 fl oz) can
   coconut milk
1 vanilla pod
200 ml (7 fl oz) milk
4 egg yolks
125 g (4 oz) caster sugar
25 ml (5 tsp) powdered
   gelatine
30-45 ml (2-3 tbsp) coconut
   liqueur
150 ml (¼ pint) double
   cream
FRUIT SAUCE
1 large ripe mango, about
   450 g (1 lb)
juice of 1 large orange
juice of 1 lime
2 ripe wrinkly passion fruit
icing sugar, to taste
TO DECORATE
mint sprigs
finely shredded orange and
   lime rinds (optional)

PREPARATION TIME
30 minutes, plus chilling
COOKING TIME
15-20 minutes
FREEZING
Suitable: Sauce only

500 CALS PER SERVING

1. Pour the coconut milk into a non-aluminium saucepan and whisk well to mix. Split the vanilla pod lengthways and scrape the black seeds into the coconut milk. Stir in the milk, heat to boiling point, then remove from the heat.

2. Whisk the egg yolks and sugar together until pale and fluffy. Pour on the coconut milk and stir well. Return to the pan and cook over a gentle heat, stirring all the time, for about 15 minutes until slightly thickened to the consistency of double cream; do not boil or it will curdle. Strain into a bowl, cover the surface with damp greaseproof paper to prevent a skin forming, and allow to cool.

3. Put 50 ml (2 fl oz) cold water in a small bowl and sprinkle on the gelatine. Leave until softened and sponge-like, then stand the bowl in a pan of simmering water and stir occasionally until dissolved. Stir thoroughly into the cold custard with the coconut liqueur. Chill for 15-20 minutes until the custard begins to thicken; check and stir every 5 minutes.

4. Lightly oil six 150 ml (¼ pint) individual moulds. Whip cream until holding soft peaks, then fold into the custard. Carefully spoon into the moulds and tap each one on the work surface to knock out large air bubbles. Cover and chill for at least 2-3 hours until set.

5. To make the sauce, peel the mango and cut the flesh away from the stone. Place in a blender or food processor with the orange and lime juices. Purée until smooth, then pass through a sieve into a bowl. Halve the passion fruit and scoop out the seeds into the mango sauce. Stir in icing sugar to taste. If the sauce is a little thick, thin with a little more orange juice. Chill.

6. To serve, run a thin-bladed knife around each bavarois and invert onto a dessert plate. Spoon over a little of the sauce and pour the rest around the bavarois. Decorate with mint and shreds of orange and lime rinds, if desired.

TECHNIQUE

Halve the passion fruit and scoop out the seeds and pulp into the mango sauce.

PISTACHIO PRALINE FLOATING ISLANDS

Soft pillows of poached meringue speckled with green and amber pieces of pistachio praline – floating on a lake of delicate pale yellow custard – makes an impressive dessert. The praline can, of course, be made well ahead and stored in an airtight container until required.

SERVES 4-6

PRALINE
50 g (2 oz) unskinned
   pistachio nuts
50 g (2 oz) caster sugar
FLOATING ISLANDS
2 eggs, separated
150 g (5 oz) caster sugar
300 ml (½ pint) single
   cream
300 ml (½ pint) milk

PREPARATION TIME
30 minutes, plus chilling
COOKING TIME
18-20 minutes
FREEZING
Not suitable

520-350 CALS PER SERVING

1. First make the praline. Lightly oil a baking sheet. Put the pistachios and sugar in a small heavy-based saucepan over a gentle heat and stir with a metal spoon until the sugar melts and begins to caramelise. Continue to cook until the mixture is a deep brown colour, then immediately pour onto the oiled baking sheet. Leave to cool completely, then pound to a coarse powder in a food processor or blender.

2. To make the meringue, whisk the egg whites in a bowl until they form soft peaks. Gradually whisk in 75 g (3 oz) of the caster sugar until the mixture is very stiff and shiny. Quickly and carefully fold in all but 30 ml (2 tbsp) of the praline.

3. Place the cream, milk and remaining sugar in a medium saucepan and bring to a gentle simmer. Spoon 5-6 small rounds of meringue mixture into the pan and cook gently for 2-3 minutes, or until they have doubled in size and are quite firm to the touch. Remove with a slotted spoon and drain on kitchen paper. Repeat with the remaining mixture: you should have 12-18 meringues, depending on size.

4. Whisk the egg yolks into the poaching liquid. Heat gently, stirring all the time, until the custard thickens slightly to the consistency of double cream; do not allow to boil or it will curdle.

5. Strain the custard into a serving dish, or individual dishes, and position the meringues on top. Cool, then chill for 30 minutes. Serve sprinkled with the remaining praline.

NOTE: The meringues can be made a few hours in advance and kept floating on the custard. Sprinkle with praline just before serving.

VARIATIONS

Use hazelnuts or almonds instead of the pistachios. Add a pinch of cinnamon or nutmeg to the custard.

TECHNIQUE

As soon as the caramel and nut mixture turns a deep brown colour, carefully pour it onto the oiled baking sheet.

BROWN SUGAR MERINGUES WITH RASPBERRY SAUCE

Generous clouds of meringue are filled with whipped cream and sliced peaches and served on a sharp ruby red sauce. Demerara sugar adds a slight caramel flavour to the meringues and colours them a pretty, pale beige. Use nectarines instead of peaches, or strawberries, if you prefer.

SERVES 6

MERINGUE
4 egg whites
125 g (4 oz) granulated sugar
125 g (4 oz) demerara sugar
RASPBERRY SAUCE
450 g (1 lb) fresh or frozen raspberries, thawed
30 ml (2 tbsp) lemon juice
icing sugar, to taste
30 ml (2 tbsp) kirsch
TO ASSEMBLE
2-3 ripe peaches
15 ml (1 tbsp) kirsch
300 ml (½ pint) double cream

PREPARATION TIME
35 minutes, plus cooling
COOKING TIME
3-4 hours
FREEZING
Not suitable

375 CALS PER SERVING

1. Preheat the oven to 110°C (225 °F) Mark ¼. Put the egg whites in a large bowl and whisk until very stiff but not dry. Gradually whisk in the combined sugars, spoonful by spoonful, allowing the mixture to become very stiff between each addition.

2. Line a baking sheet with non-stick baking parchment. Spoon or pipe about 12 meringues onto the parchment. Bake in the oven for 3-4 hours until thoroughly dried out.

3. Remove the meringues from the oven and leave to cool on the parchment. Carefully lift off when cool and store in an airtight container until required.

4. To make the raspberry sauce, place the raspberries in a blender or food processor with the lemon juice and icing sugar to taste. Work to a purée, then pass through a sieve to remove any seeds. Stir in the kirsch, cover and chill in the refrigerator.

5. Immerse the peaches in a bowl of boiling water for 20 seconds to loosen the skins. Lift out and plunge into cold water to stop further cooking. Peel off the skins. Halve the peaches and remove the stones. Slice neatly and sprinkle with 15 ml (1 tbsp) kirsch.

6. To serve, whip the cream until it just holds soft peaks. Spoon the cream onto six of the meringues. Arrange the sliced peaches on top and sandwich together with the remaining meringues. Place on individual serving plates and pour over the raspberry sauce. Serve immediately.

NOTE: The secret to making these meringues is to whisk the egg whites initially until very stiff and to whisk until stiff between each addition of sugar. Do not add the sugar too quickly, or the meringue will become thin.

TECHNIQUE

Shape the meringue into large ovals, using two tablespoons and place on a baking sheet lined with non-stick baking parchment.

RHUBARB AND GINGER ICE CREAM

Rhubarb and ginger are a favourite combination in my native Scotland where everyone's grandmother makes the best rhubarb and ginger jam! The ice cream can be pale pink or green depending on the type of rhubarb – adding a drop of natural food colouring enhances the colour. Dainty ginger biscuits are the perfect complement.

SERVES 4

350 g (12 oz) trimmed
   rhubarb stalks
50 g (2 oz) sugar, or to taste
75 g (3 oz) stem ginger in
   syrup, drained and syrup
   reserved
150 ml (¼ pint) single
   cream
150 ml (¼ pint) double
   cream
2 egg yolks
GINGER BISCUITS
50 g (2 oz) butter
25 g (1 oz) caster sugar
75 g (3 oz) plain white flour
5 ml (1 tsp) ground ginger
extra caster sugar, for
   dusting
TO DECORATE
a little chopped stem ginger
   in syrup, drained

PREPARATION TIME
45 minutes, plus freezing
COOKING TIME
40 minutes
FREEZING
Suitable: Ice cream only

495 CALS PER SERVING

1. Cut the rhubarb into chunks and place in a saucepan with the sugar and 30 ml (2 tbsp) ginger syrup. Cover, bring to the boil, lower the heat and simmer for 15-20 minutes until very tender. Allow to cool slightly, then purée in a blender or food processor until smooth. Cool. Chop the ginger finely and add to the rhubarb purée. Chill.

2. Pour the two creams into a saucepan and bring to the boil. Whisk the egg yolks together in a bowl, then whisk in the scalded creams. Return to the pan. Stir the custard over a very gentle heat for about 15 minutes until thickened to the consistency of double cream. Remove from the heat, cover the surface with greaseproof paper to prevent a skin forming and allow to cool, then chill.

3. Stir the custard into the chilled rhubarb mixture, then taste and add more ginger syrup if necessary. Freeze in an ice cream machine, according to the manufacturer's directions. Alternatively, turn into a freezerproof container, cover and freeze until firm, whisking occasionally (see note).

4. To make the ginger biscuits, cream the butter and sugar together in a bowl. Sift the flour and ginger together over the mixture, then beat in thoroughly.

When the mixture forms a ball, knead lightly, then roll out on a floured surface to a 3 mm (⅛ inch) thickness. Using a biscuit cutter, cut out shapes and place on a baking sheet. Chill for 15 minutes.

5. Preheat the oven to 190°C (375°F) Mark 5, then bake the biscuits for 10-15 minutes. Sprinkle with caster sugar whilst still warm. Leave to cool.

6. Scoop the ice cream into serving dishes and top with a little chopped ginger. Serve with the ginger biscuits.

NOTE: If you are not using an ice cream maker it is important to whisk the mixture periodically during freezing to break down the ice crystals and ensure a smooth-textured result.

TECHNIQUE

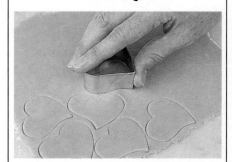

Using a small heart-shaped or round cutter, stamp out the biscuits.